WELCOME TO BAYOU TOWN!

WELCOME TO BAYOU TOWN!

By Chérie D. Schadler

**Illustrated by
Ann Biedenharn Jones**

PELICAN PUBLISHING COMPANY
Gretna 1996

The word "Pelican" and the depiction of a pelican are trademarks
of Pelican Publishing Company, Inc., and are registered
in the U.S. Patent and Trademark Office.

Library of Congress Cataloging-in-Publication Data

Schadler, Chérie D.
    Welcome to Bayou Town! / by Chérie D. Schadler ; illustrations by Ann
Biedenharn Jones.
        p.   cm.
    Summary: A trip to Bayou Town brings adventures with many animal and human
friends.
    ISBN 1-56554-161-8 (hc : alk. paper)
    [1. Bayous—Fiction. 2. Animals—Fiction. 3. Louisiana—Fiction. 4. Stories in
rhyme.] I. Jones, Ann Biedenharn, ill. II. Title.
PZ8.3.S2875Wj 1996
[E]—dc20   96-15572
                                                                                                    CIP
                                                                                                    AC

Printed in Singapore

Published by Pelican Publishing Company, Inc.
1101 Monroe Street, Gretna, Louisiana 70053

For my Heavenly Father
*(through whom all things **have** been made possible [Mark 9:23]);*
my best friend, Papa-Ron;
my precious son, Joey;
and Mom and Dad

ACKNOWLEDGMENTS

The success of Bayou Town℠ has resulted from a cooperation of faith and support. I would like to express sincere gratitude to family; friends; librarians; educators; event coordinators; Bookends Book Store; the Mississippi Arts Commission; the Hancock County Beautification Committee, Chamber of Commerce, and Board of Supervisors; the Mississippi Marine Trash Task Force; REACH TV; the *Sea Coast Echo;* WLOX-Channel 13; Pelican Publishing Company; and the many others who have made it possible to bring Bayou Town℠ before the children.

CHARACTERS

Narrator, Acadian girl
Mr. Boudreaux (Boo-droh), mayor of Bayou Town
Miss Marie, wife of Mr. Boudreaux
Toby, son of Mr. Boudreaux and Miss Marie
Alfons, alligator, Boudreaux family pet

I know a place not very far away
    where we can dance with crawfish and play
    "Alligator-Keep-Away"!
We can fish on the *bayou* and climb the live oak trees.
    I'd be very pleased to show you if you'd like to come with me.

It's just down the *levee* from the muddy Mississip,
  just a hop and a waddle and a scurry and a skip . . .
So grab your old straw hat, and your best cane pole,
  for my little *pirogue* is all ready to go!
I'm on my way there now, you see,
  to buy some spice that my mama needs.

So let's pole through the grasses, and the tall cattails,
past the cypress trees, and the 'possum trails.
And if you'll keep real still, and try not to wiggle,
I'll pole the boat beneath the moss
and give your ears a little tickle!

Shhh . . . here in the swamp the animals are wise.
They blend with the thicket and search with their eyes.
Not a move do they make, not a sound do they say,
when not far away Mr. Alligator plays!

Hey, look . . . straight up ahead, upon that *pier*, beyond that shed.

   We're almost there—let's pull around.
See? There's the sign, Welcome to Bayou Town!

   Hello there, Mama 'Possum and Mr. Raccoon.
Shhh . . . good day, Brown Pelican.

   Hope you catch that catfish soon!

Here on the bayou, the buildings stand on piers:
 businesses, church, and schoolhouse . . . all here.
But today we're on an errand to fill my mama's sack,
 so we'll tie up right here at Mr. Boudreaux's Seafood Shack.
He's the mayor of Bayou Town.
 He's friends with everyone for miles around!

"Hello, Mr. Boudreaux, I'm back again.
    This time I brought a special friend.
Mama sent me to buy crab boil, some of your very special
blend."
    "*Aieee!* Hello dere, *chère*. Na' y'all c'mon, pull up a chair.
I was jes' cookin' up some *filé gumbo*.
    Dem crabs are really snappin', you know!"

"Mr. Boudreaux, watch out! That crab's too close."
"*Oooeee! Dat crab, he pinch' ma' nose!*
I sho' don' t'ink dat gumbo's done.
I'm gonna tole you, ma' fren, I'd betta' stir it some.

Ya yeee, ya yaaa, bon appétit, c'est vrai,
Ya yeee, ya yooo, c'est bon filé gumbo!"

Hey, look . . . up in the clubhouse . . . there.
Do you see that pirate with the brown curly hair?
That's Toby—he's Mr. Boudreaux's son.
His pretend pirate games are lots of fun.

"Ahoy there, Toby, meet my new friend!"
"Ahoy, ye mates! Glad to see you again.
Did you come to the Kids' Club to play with me?
I'm a pirate today—I'm *Jean Lafitte*."

"I'm tracking an alligator who's been up to his pranks.
He ate up my treasure without saying, 'Thanks!'
But we'll find him soon if we stick to the trail
of the marshmallow goo that stuck to his tail. Yarrr!"

"Ooo-yiiieee! Ma' po' onion!
   Quick, quick, Boudreaux, Alfons is on de run!"
"Oh no, I hear ma' wife, Marie!
   Ma' pet alligata, he make mischief, I see.
I betta' catch him, me. *I'm comin', Ma-rieee!*"

Miss Marie's garden is something *special* to see.
It's just around back—*quick,* let's take a peek!
See, there's her okra, hot peppers, Creole tomatoes, and beans,
her poor green onions and mustard greens.
And along that line, that's her *mirliton* vine.

"Ahoy, ye mates, what's that green thing there?
  It's got teeth from ear to ear!"
Chomp! Hey! He stole my hat—Alfons wants to play!
  "*Yarrr!* Catch him, somebody.
  It's *Alligator-Keep-Away!*"

He's down in the hyacinths.

No . . . he's under the trees!

"Hoo-ya-yeee! I t'ink I see
him down in dem knees."

"He shouldn't get far with four on his tail.

Yuck! But he's slippery and slimy,
and fast on the trail."

"I think Miss Marie's got him behind the schoolhouse."
"Nope! Thar he blows! Your hat is *still* in his mouth."

"He's down in dem t'istles. Na' he's up on dat pier!"

"Shhh . . . Papa, I can see him in my scope from up over here.

He's up on the fence—I think he might jump."

"*Quick, quick, net him, t-boy, befo' he hit dat . . .*"

Thump!

Whew, that was a close one. He almost got away!
But my hat is now safe, at least safe for today.
"Na' I'm gonna tole you, ma' fren, 'tho he sneaky dat way,
man, it make fo' big fun, when Alfons wants to play. *Aieee!*"

Whack! Ouch! The mosquitoes are coming; the sun's going down.
   I suppose that it's time to leave Bayou Town.
It's always sad to say good-bye to friends,
   but the happy part is, we can visit again!

"*Ooo, ma' chère!* Na' we almos' fo'got
dis sack o' crab boil fo' you mama's big pot.
Quick, quick na', hun, don' let suppa' get cole.
You mama, she'll be callin',
so make hase wit' you pole!"
"Oh, *merci*, Miss Marie."

"So long, Toby, Mr. Boudreaux, . . . and Alfons too!
It's sure been a special day here with you."

"Na', ma' frenz, dis day
    you make special when you came 'roun',
to share a smile wit' me,
    Mr. Boudreaux, in Bayou Town.
So, may you keep dat song in you hawt, an' dat smile on you
face.
    May you spread it wit' kindness all ova' de place.
An' may all you journeys be happy an' safe, ma' frenz,
    'til you pass a good trip an' come see me again! Yes? *Aieee!*"

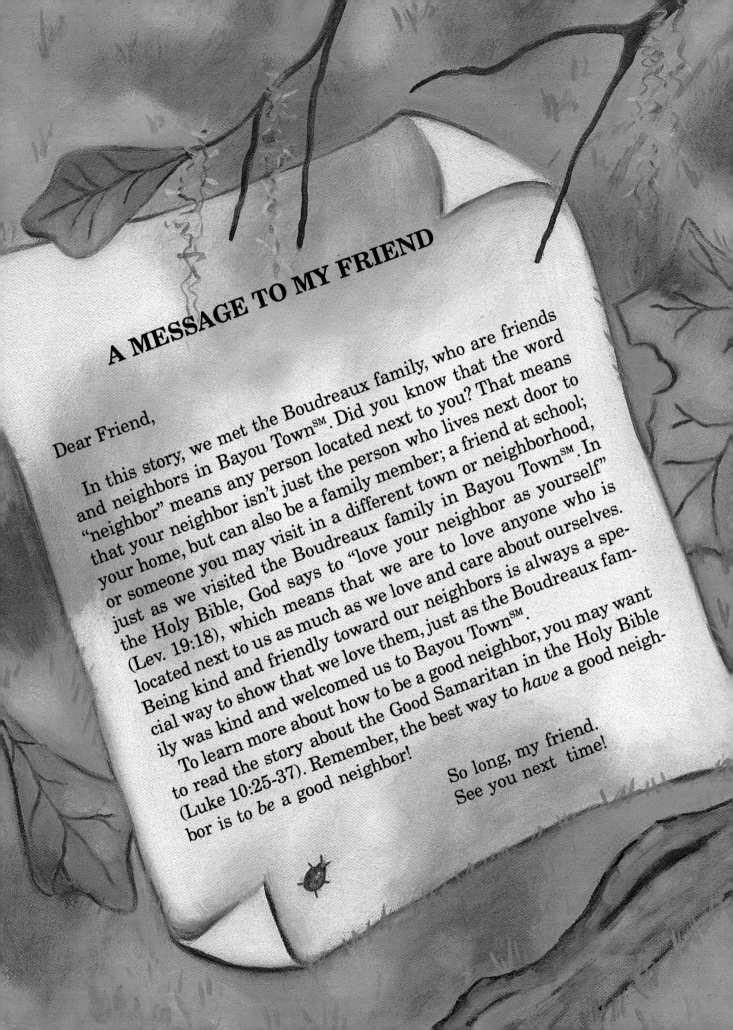

A MESSAGE TO MY FRIEND

Dear Friend,

In this story, we met the Boudreaux family, who are friends and neighbors in Bayou Town℠. Did you know that the word "neighbor" means any person located next to you? That means that your neighbor isn't just the person who lives next door to your home, but can also be a family member; a friend at school; or someone you may visit in a different town or neighborhood, just as we visited the Boudreaux family in Bayou Town℠. In the Holy Bible, God says to "love your neighbor as yourself" (Lev. 19:18), which means that we are to love anyone who is located next to us as much as we love and care about ourselves. Being kind and friendly toward our neighbors is always a special way to show that we love them, just as the Boudreaux family was kind and welcomed us to Bayou Town℠.

To learn more about how to be a good neighbor, you may want to read the story about the Good Samaritan in the Holy Bible (Luke 10:25-37). Remember, the best way to *have* a good neighbor is to *be* a good neighbor!

So long, my friend.
See you next time!

GLOSSARY

Cajun-French	Approximate English Pronunciation	English
bayou	by-you	a marshy, sluggish body of water
bon appétit, c'est vrai	bohn ah-pay-tee, say vray	good eating, that's true
c'est bon filé gumbo	say boh(n) fee-lay gum-boh	that's good thick, seasoned soup
chère	shehr	dear (feminine spelling)
filé gumbo	fee-lay gum-boh	thick, seasoned soup
Jean Lafitte	Zhahn Lah-feet	was a pirate of south Louisiana
levee	leh-vee	built-up riverbank or bayou bank
merci	mehr-see	thank you
mirliton	muhr-lih-tahn	vegetable pear
pier	peer	boardwalk over water
pirogue	pee-rohg	dugout or canoe made from a cypress log
t-boy	tee-boy	little boy
ya yeee, ya yaaa	yah-yee yah-yah	song, like "la-la-la"
ya yeee, ya yooo	yah-yee yah-yoh	song, like "la-la-la"